W9-AVR-212
Renewals: (847) 923-3158

DATE DUE			

This book belongs to:

_____

_____

_____

First published by Walker Books, Ltd., 87 Vauxhall Walk, London SE11 5HJ

Copyright © 2001 by Lucy Cousins
Lucy Cousins font copyright © 2001 by Lucy Cousins

Based on the audiovisual series "Maisy." A King Rollo Films production for Universal
Pictures International Visual Programming. Original script by Andrew Brenner.
Illustrated in the style of Lucy Cousins by King Rollo Films Ltd.

First U.S. edition 2001

Library of Congress Catalog Card Number 00-111827

ISBN 978-0-7636-1612-0 (hardcover)
ISBN 978-0-7636-1613-7 (paperback)

12 13 14 15 SWT 25 24 23 22 21 20 19

Printed in Dongguan, Guangdong, China

This book was typeset in Lucy Cousins.
The illustrations were done in gouache.

Candlewick Press
99 Dover Street
Somerville, Massachusetts 02144

visit us at www.candlewick.com

Doctor Maisy

Lucy Cousins

CANDLEWICK PRESS

Hello, Doctor Maisy.
Hello, Nurse Tallulah.
Let's play hospital!

Tallulah listens to Maisy's heartbeat. That tickles!

Panda is sick today.
Maisy listens to
his heartbeat.
Thump, thump,
thump!

Maisy takes Panda's temperature.

Oh, no.
Panda has a fever.

Panda needs to rest. Maisy carries him up the stairs.

Night-night, Panda.
Get well soon.

Tallulah calls
from downstairs.
Maisy! Maisy!

Maisy runs
down the stairs.

Careful,
not too fast!

Crash!
Maisy bumps
into Tallulah.

Ouch!

Tallulah wraps
Maisy's nose
in a bandage.

That's better!
Bye-bye, Nurse Tallulah.
Bye-bye, Doctor Maisy.

Lucy Cousins is one of today's most acclaimed author-illustrators of children's books. Her unique titles instantly engage babies, toddlers, and preschoolers with their childlike simplicity and bright colors. And the winsome exploits of characters like Maisy reflect the adventures that young children have every day.

Lucy admits that illustration comes more easily to her than writing, which tends to work around the drawings. "I draw by heart," she says. "I think of what children would like by going back to my own childlike instincts." And what instincts! Lucy Cousins now has more than thirteen million books in print, from cloth and picture books to irresistible pull-the-tab and lift-the-flap books.